EGMONT
We bring stories to life

First published in Great Britain in 2015 by Egmont UK Limited,
The Yellow Building, 1 Nicholas Road, London W11 4AN.

Written by: Kate Graham
Designed by: Claire Yeo and Anthony Duke

© 2015 Disney Enterprises, Inc.

ISBN 978 1 4052 8058 7
63224/1
Printed in Italy

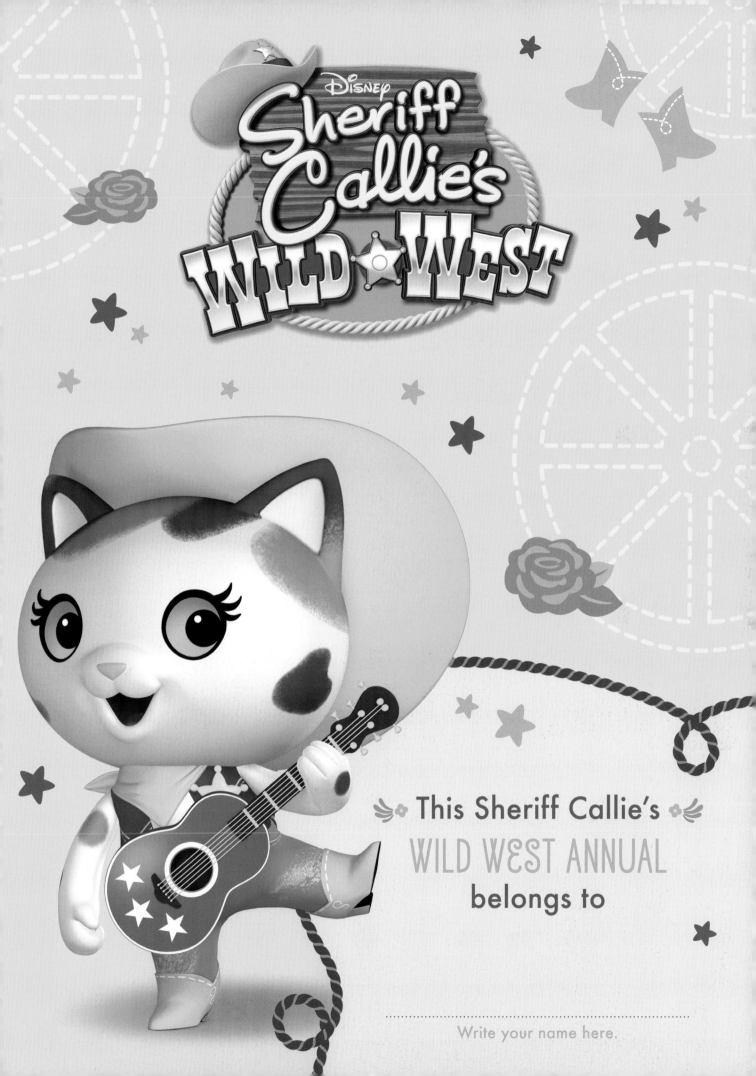

This Sheriff Callie's
WILD WEST ANNUAL
belongs to

Write your name here.

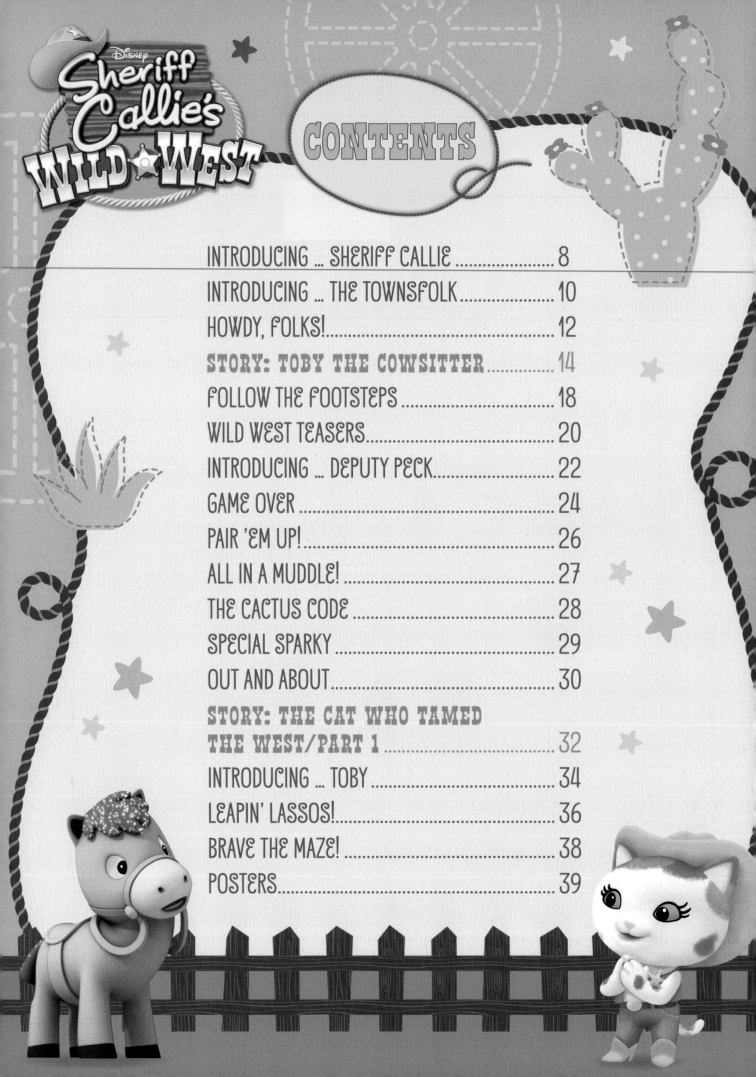

CONTENTS

Introducing ... SHERIFF CALLIE

KITTY CAT FACTS

- Sheriff Callie is brave, smart and kind.

- She watches over the Wild West town of Nice and Friendly Corners. The folk there feel safe and happy when this little cat is around.

- Deputy Peck, Toby and Sparky are Sheriff Callie's trusted team of helpers.

- Sheriff Callie wears a pink cowgirl hat and matching boots – and is never to be seen without her gold star badge.

- She has a magic noodle lasso that comes in mighty handy when there's trouble in town!

- Listen out for music when Callie's about: she plays purr-fectly fine tunes on her guitar.

- Hear her yell: 'Sweet sassafras!'

Prize Trail

This trail leads to something Sheriff Callie loves.

What is it? →

8

MEET THE CHARACTERS WHO LIVE IN NICE AND FRIENDLY CORNERS.

SPARKY

Who: Sheriff Callie's loyal pony

Appearance: Blue coat and a sparkly mane

Known for: Galloping at top speed when chasing baddies!

ELLA COWBELLE

Who: Cow who runs the town's Milk Saloon

Appearance: Big, blue eyes with an apron to match

Known for: Serving up the best milkshakes for miles around

UNCLE BUN

Who: Chatty rabbit and owner of the general store

Appearance: Grey and furry with gold-rimmed spectacles

Known for: Loving carrots and playing board games with Tio Tortuga

CLEMENTINE

Who: Deputy Peck's mule

Appearance: Stubborn expression

Known for: Being slow and laid-back

TIO TORTUGA

Who: Wise and kind tortoise

Appearance: Lots of wrinkles – he's 110 years old!

Known for: His Spanish accent and taking naps

PRISCILLA SKUNK

Who: Well-dressed skunk

Appearance: Rather beautiful, as skunks go

Known for: Not being smelly (unlike her cousin, Farmer Stinky!)

Wild West Talk

Trace over the letters to show a Nice and Friendly greeting.

Howdy

Howdy Folks!

TOBY

SPARKY

Shadow Match

Can you match each character to the correct shadow?

We've found Sparky's for you!

a

b

12

SAY, IT'S SHERIFF CALLIE AND ALL HER FRIENDS WHO HELP KEEP NICE AND FRIENDLY CORNERS A HAPPY TOWN.

SHERIFF CALLIE

DEPUTY PECK

ⓒ

ⓓ

I Spy

Clementine, Deputy Peck's mule, is hiding.

Can you spot her?

Answers on page 66.

13

TOBY THE COWSITTER

Ella has created a new milkshake.

It's the yummiest milkshake I've ever made. And it only costs a nickel!

Everyone races into Ella's Saloon to order their shakes.

But when Toby empties his piggy bank at home, there is only a pebble and two marbles inside.

Boy, oh boy! I love milkshakes! All I need is a nickel!

Aw, now what am I gonna do?

Just then, two farmers walk up leading two cows. "Here's two nickels if you babysit these here cows," they say to Toby.

Toby is so excited. He runs straight back to Ella's Saloon and orders two more milkshakes!

As Toby drinks his milkshakes, three more farmers walk in. "Anyone here wanna look after our cows? We'll pay a nickel each."

Meanwhile, Sheriff Callie and Deputy Peck step out of the jailhouse.

Toby appears and explains about looking after the cows in exchange for the nickels. He takes a huge slurp of milkshake.

Leapin' lassos!

Who's supposed to be watching these cows?

SLUUUURRRRPPP!

Oh dear, I'm not meant to do that ...

Suddenly, there's a crazy cow stampede! The cows trample through town and then head for the water tower. Sheriff Callie jumps on Sparky.

If they knock down that tower, they'll flood the whole town. Time for my lasso to work its magic!

Sheriff Callie manages to throw her lasso over the cows and they skid to a halt. She's saved the day! But the cows have left the town in a terrible mess.

Toby feels ashamed. He was so excited about the milkshakes that he'd forgotten the promises he made.

From now on, I promise to keep my promises. And I promise to clean up this mess, too!

Forgetting you've made a promise is just as bad as breaking a promise.

THE END

True or False?

Toby is peeking out from behind a tree.

FINISH

Wild West Teasers

1 Which of these items does not belong to Sheriff Callie?

a
b
c
d
e

2 Trace over the letters to reveal one of Sheriff Callie's favourite drinks.

Which trail will lead Deputy Peck to his best buddy, Toby?

Join the dots to complete Sheriff Callie's outfit, then colour it in.

Can you spot some more lassos like this one looping around on the page?

Answers on page 66.

21

Introducing ... DEPUTY PECK

DEPUTY SHERIFF
FACTS

- Woodpecker Deputy Peck is Sheriff Callie's loyal and trusty deputy.

- He has heaps of energy and is super-keen to do his job properly. Sheriff Callie steps in if he gets a bit too bossy ...

- Peck rides an easy-going mule called Clementine. His best pal is Toby the cactus.

- Just like his boss, Deputy Peck wears a gold star badge. Check out his blue neckerchief and cowboy boots for Wild West style.

- Peck's favourite food is Trail Mix. He'll happily peck away at corn and prairie peppers, too.

- His catchphrase is: 'Ouchity Ouch Ouch Ouch!'

Hoppin' Hats!

Which hat belongs to Deputy Peck?

Tick the box.

(a)

(b)

BRIGHTEN UP **DEPUTY PECK** BY COLOURING HIM IN.

Game Over

THE RAIN AND WIND IS SPOILING SHERIFF CALLIE AND TOBY'S CARD GAME. COUNT THE **BLUE** AND **RED** CARDS THAT HAVE BLOWN AWAY.

Blue [ ]

Red [ ]

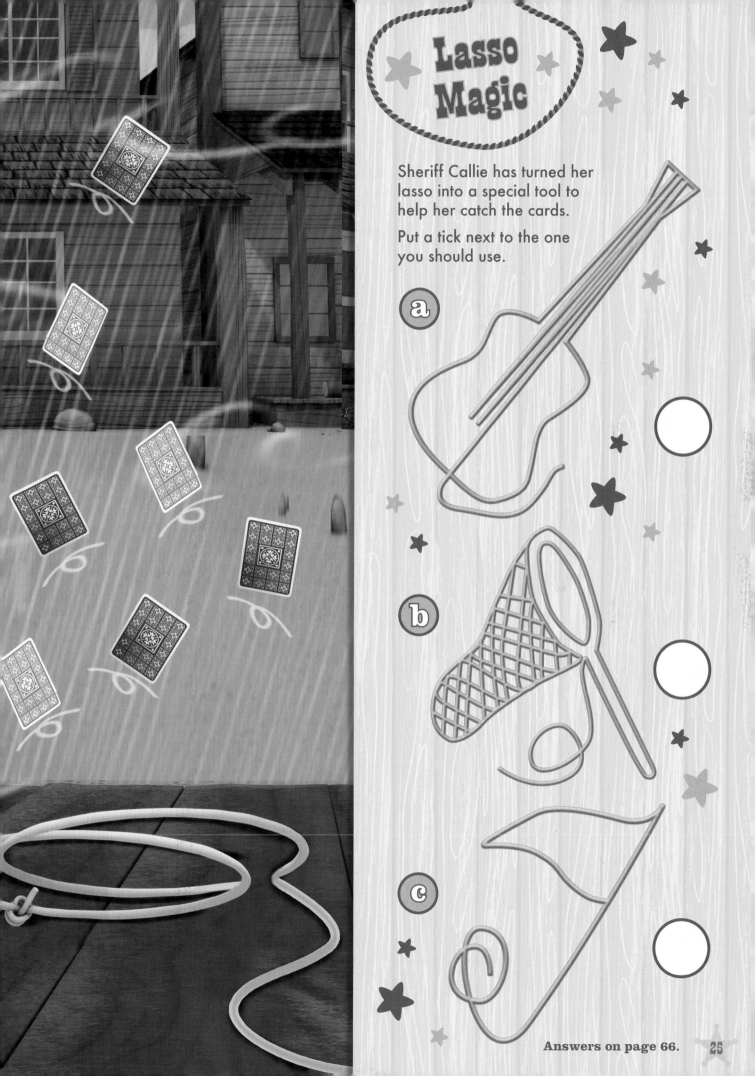

Lasso Magic

Sheriff Callie has turned her lasso into a special tool to help her catch the cards.

Put a tick next to the one you should use.

a

b

c

Pair 'Em Up!

CAN YOU PUT THESE DESERT PLANTS INTO **MATCHING PAIRS?** DRAW A LINE TO CONNECT EACH PAIR. THERE IS AN ODD ONE OUT.

a

b

c

d

e

f

g

Colour Check

What colour is the rose?

Blue

Pink

Yellow

Answers on page 66.

All in a Muddle!

LOOK CAREFULLY AT THE TOP PICTURE OF **SHERIFF CALLIE** PLAYING HER GUITAR. THEN, NUMBER THE JUMBLED UP SECTIONS BELOW SO THAT THEY MAKE THE SAME PICTURE.

1
2
3
4
5
6

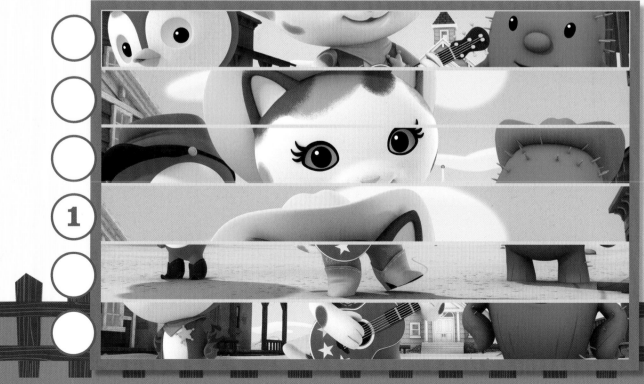

1

Answers on page 66.

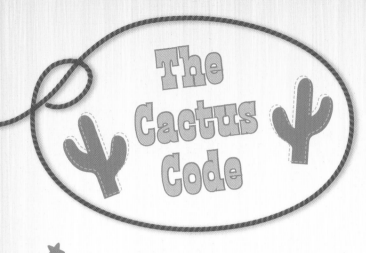

The Cactus Code

DO YOU KNOW WHAT **TOBY'S** FULL NAME IS? HE'S WRITTEN IT HERE USING A PICTURE CODE. WORK IT OUT BY WRITING THE RIGHT LETTER UNDER EACH PICTURE.

Answers on page 66.

Special Sparky

SHERIFF CALLIE TAKES VERY GOOD CARE OF SPARKY, HER HORSE. COLOUR IN THE DOTTED SECTIONS OF THE DRAWINGS TO REVEAL WHAT SHE HAS FOR HIM TODAY. MATCH YOUR CRAYONS TO THE COLOUR OF THE DOTS.

Answers on page 66.

START

3

Sheriff Callie has lost
her lasso. Follow the
trail to find it.

4

Is Toby looking happy or sad?
Trace around the right face below.

Part 1

THE CAT WHO TAMED THE WEST

Long ago, there was a cowgirl named Callie. She had a horse named Sparky, and a magic noodle lasso. Callie was the bravest, bestest cowgirl in the Wild West.

One hot morning, Callie and Sparky rode off to find something nice and cool to drink. They finally came to a dirty and dusty town called Mean and Messy Corners.

Callie walked over to Ella's Saloon.

But when Callie entered, Ella yelped and hid behind the counter.

Don't be afraid. I'd just like a nice, cold glass of milk.

This looks like a mighty fine place for a drink!

Coming right up!

Just then, a milk bandit barged into the saloon.

Paws up! This is a milk raid!

Callie whipped out her magic lasso and bounced the milk bandit out of town before he could steal a drop.

Ella was so grateful she gave Callie a giant milkshake. No sooner had Callie taken a sip than two more bandits rode up.

"We're the Banjo Bandit Brothers!" shouted the big one. "Give us all yer banjos!"

The townsfolk were scared. Uncle Bun jumped inside a barrel. Tio Tortuga hid inside his shell. But one prairie dog wasn't fast enough. The big Banjo Bandit Brother grabbed his banjo and ran off!

Callie had seen enough.

Giddy up, Sparky. We've got a banjo to save!

To be continued ...

Introducing ... TOBY

HAPPY CACTUS
FACTS

- Toby the cactus is best buddies with Deputy Peck.

- He is a very happy cactus and is always looking to have fun.

- Toby rolls on a barrel when he goes on adventures with Callie and Peck.

- Being a cactus, Toby is rather spiney. The orange cowboy hat he wears fits snugly over the spines on his head!

- Toby loves dancing and he plays a good tune on the harmonica.

- He cannot resist Ella's milkshakes and he munches a lot of popcorn, too!

- When Toby's spines are a bother, he calls himself 'a pokey cowpoke'.

Odd One Out

Can you spot which barrel is the odd one out?

a

b

c

Leapin' Lassos!

MY OH MY, **SHERIFF CALLIE** IS USING HER LASSO TO SPIN APPLES IN THE AIR! HELP THEM STAY UP BY TRACING THE LOOPY CIRCLES THEY'RE MAKING.

★ Colour Check ★

Look carefully at this line of
apples. Colour in the last one
to complete the sequence.

Brave the Maze!

DEPUTY PECK HAS LOST HIS HAT! CAN YOU HELP HIM THROUGH THE MAZE TO **TOBY** AT THE OTHER END?

FINISH

START

Answers on page 66.

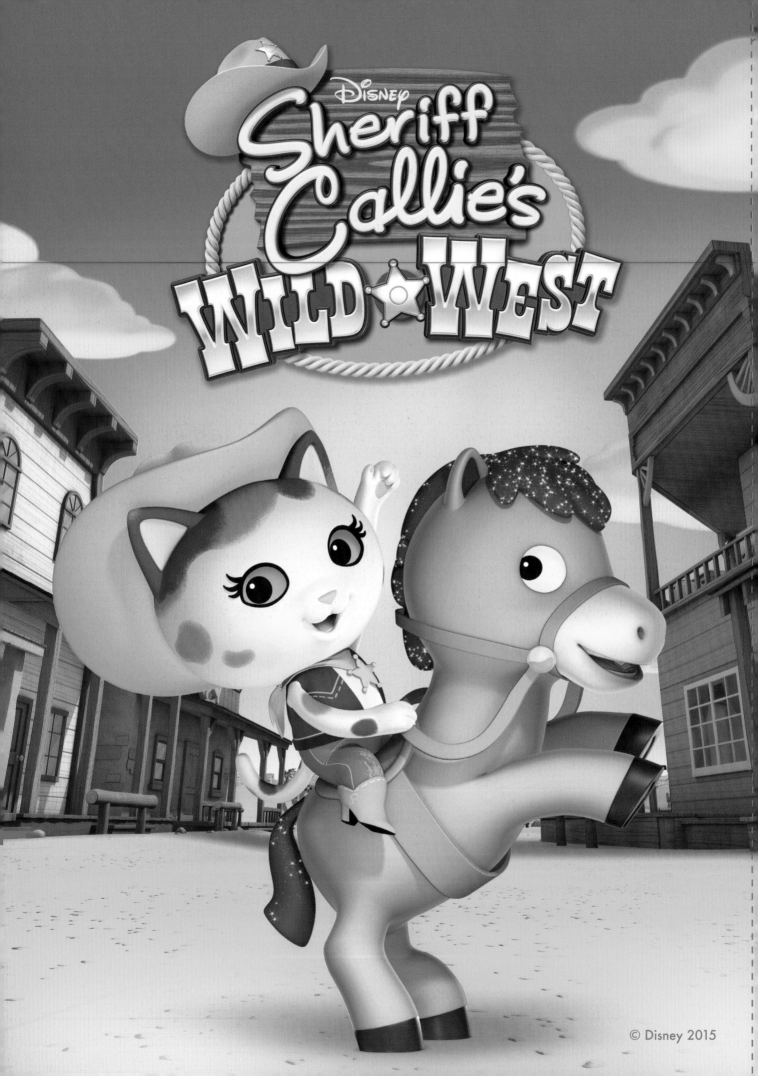

Mirror Message

DEPUTY PECK'S MESSAGE REMINDS THE FOLK OF **NICE AND FRIENDLY CORNERS** WHY CALLIE IS THE BEST SHERIFF EVER. BUT HE'S WRITTEN IT BACKWARDS! USE A MIRROR TO DISCOVER THE MESSAGE!

FRIEND TO ALL!

Answers on page 66.

Collect the Corn!

CALLIE WANTS PECK AND TOBY TO PICK UP THE CORN THAT THE WIND HAS BLOWN ALL OVER THE PLACE. PLAY THE GAME AND JOIN IN THE FUN.

START

How to play:

You will need two counters and a dice. Take turns with a friend to roll the dice and move along the path. When you land on an ear of corn, tick your scoreboard. The first player to check off all the corn is the winner.

PLAYER 1

5

6 MOVE ON 3 SPACES

7

8

9

10

11

13 12

14

GO BACK 2 SPACES

15

17 16

PLAYER 2

43

You are Invited ...

SALOON PARTY

IT'S PARTY TIME IN NICE AND FRIENDLY CORNERS AND **SHERIFF CALLIE** NEEDS TO SEND OUT THE INVITATIONS. USE THE SQUARES TO COMPLETE THE DRAWINGS, THEN COLOUR IN THE DESIGN.

Party Time!

THE SALOON IS DECORATED FOR THE TOWN FAIR. HOW MANY MILKSHAKES CAN YOU SPOT IN THE PICTURE?

Colour in the balloons so that everyone sees them!

Answers on page 66.

45

TOBY BRAVES THE BULLY

Toby is excited. He has a new and important job. He's the newspaper delivery cactus for Nice and Friendly Corners. And he gets to ride a scooter, too!

Sheriff Callie has another job for Toby. Belinda Bulldog is visiting and Callie wants Toby to be friendly and helpful to her son, Bradley Bulldog.

Bradley is out to make trouble though. He snatches some of the newspapers out of Toby's bag.

Toby wants to get on with his job. He scoots down an alley to deliver some papers, leaving Bradley behind.

But Bradley Bulldog is determined to make mischief. He throws the newspapers he stole from Toby up in the air.

I'm not going to let Bradley spoil my first day at work.

This will give Toby something to think about!

What a mess! Toby is so busy clearing up all the newspapers that he doesn't realise what Bradley is up to …

Naughty Bradley has taken Toby's scooter and is whizzing away on it!

Wheeee, this is fun!

47

Now Toby is really miserable. He can't do his job. It will take too long to deliver the newspapers without his scooter.

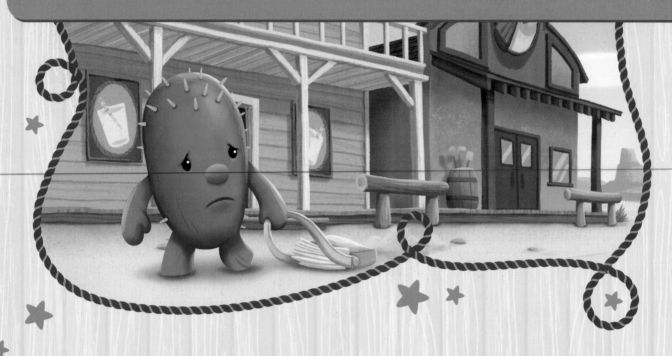

Sheriff Callie and Deputy Peck have just discovered what's going on. They aren't happy ...

You must tell Bradley to stop being a bully and be nice, Toby!

OK, I'll be as brave as a cactus can be.

Toby goes looking for Bradley. But Belinda Bulldog finds her son first.

Where did you get that scooter from, Bradley?

Just then, Toby and his friends arrive on the scene. When Toby tells Bradley how he feels, Bradley feels ashamed.

I want you to stop bullying me, Bradley! It's really not nice.

Sorry, Toby. I didn't mean to make you feel bad.

Bradley realises that being Toby's friend will be much more fun than bullying him.

I'd really like to be friends with you, Toby. And maybe I can help you deliver the papers, too!

THE END

Spring Welcome!

SPRING HAS ARRIVED IN **NICE AND FRIENDLY CORNERS**. EVERYONE IS HOLDING FLOWERS TO SHOW HOW HAPPY THEY ARE!

Match and Colour

Look carefully at the big picture and find the flower each character below is holding. Then colour in all the flowers correctly.

1

2

3

4

5

Picture Puzzles

YOU'LL NEED A BEADY EYE TO WORK OUT THESE TRICKY TEASERS!

 1 Only one of these guitars is exactly the same as the guitar Callie is playing. Which one is it?

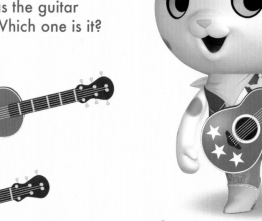

(a)

(b)

(c)

(d)

2 Draw a line connecting each pair of eyes with the character it belongs to!

(a)

(b)

(c)

TOBY

PECK

ELLA

Answers on page 66.

Heading Home

CALLIE'S BEEN OUT IN THE DESERT ALL DAY AND NOW SHE'S LONGING TO GET BACK TO TOWN. FOLLOW THE WINDING PATH AND FIND OUT WHERE SHE'S GOING – AND IF THERE'S ANYONE THERE TO KEEP HER COMPANY!

a

b

c

Answers on page 66.

Let's Go Shopping

SHERIFF CALLIE IS DOING SOME SHOPPING. HER LIST IS AT THE BOTTOM OF THE PAGE. TICK EACH ITEM WHEN YOU SPOT IT!

d

e

f

Answers on page 66.

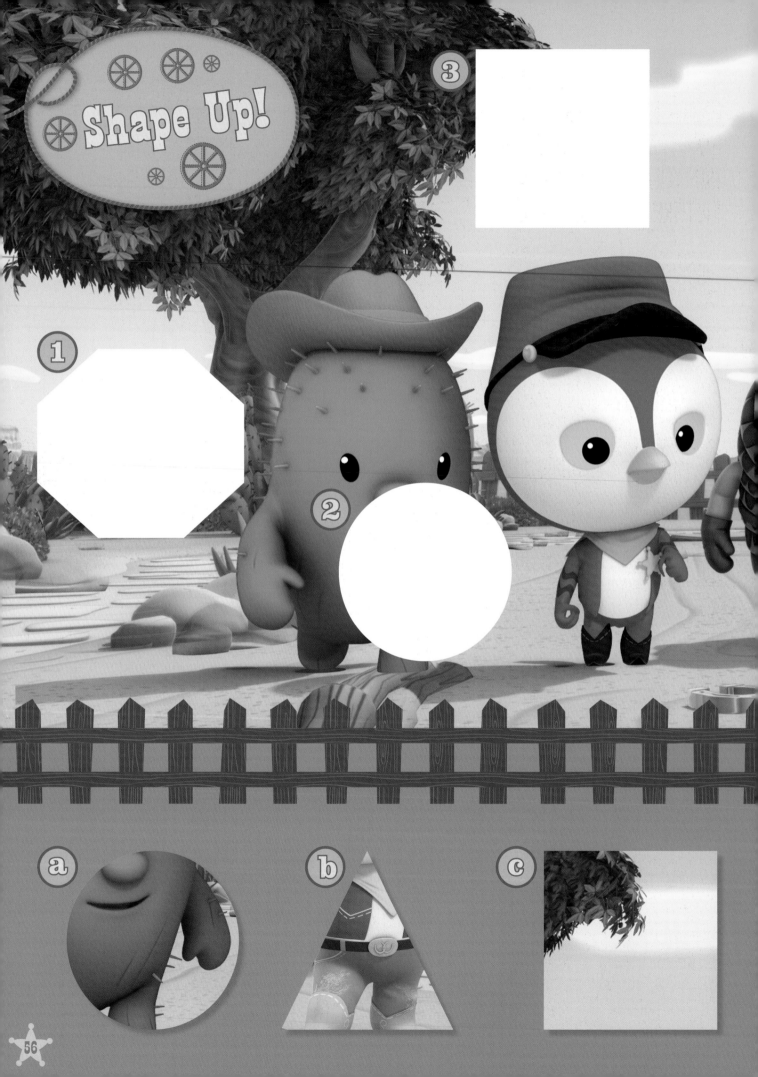

Shape Up!

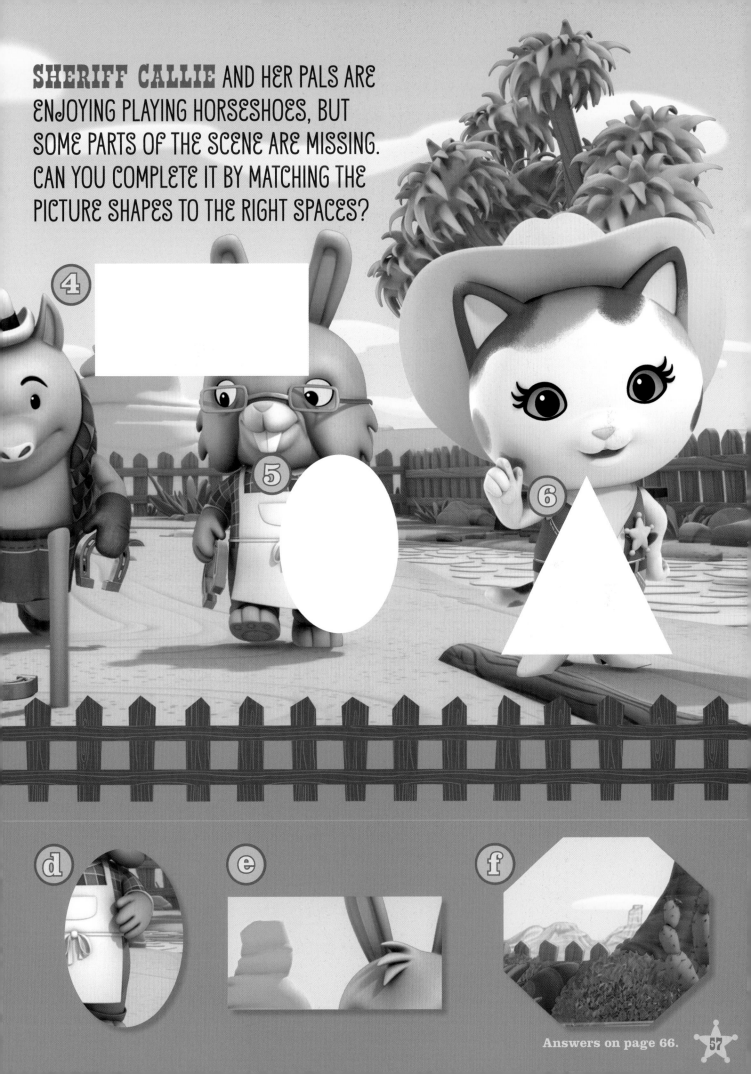

SHERIFF CALLIE AND HER PALS ARE ENJOYING PLAYING HORSESHOES, BUT SOME PARTS OF THE SCENE ARE MISSING. CAN YOU COMPLETE IT BY MATCHING THE PICTURE SHAPES TO THE RIGHT SPACES?

④

⑤

⑥

ⓓ

ⓔ

ⓕ

Answers on page 66.

THE PICTURES IN EACH ROW LOOK THE SAME, BUT ONE IS DIFFERENT. CAN YOU SPOT THE ODD ONE OUT?

1

a   b   c   d

2

a   b   c   d

3

a   b   c   d

Wheelie Easy

How many wagon wheels like this one can you count wheelin' around on this page?

58

Answers on page 66.

Colouring Fun

Sure as sunrise, Callie and Sparky need some brightening up! Get out your best colouring pens and get goin'!

THE CAT WHO TAMED THE WEST

Callie soon caught up with the Banjo Bandit Brothers. She spun her lasso so fast that the wind twirled it into a twister! Callie caught the Bandit Brothers and threw them in jail. She rescued the banjo, too!

Everybody cheered. Callie had saved the day again!

You did it! You rid our town of bad guys!

"Me?" said Callie. "Well, I'd love to."

"You'll need a nice, shiny badge," said Peck.

"I think I can handle that," Callie replied with a wink.

She took her magic lasso and spun it so high that it plucked a star right out of the sky. Then Callie pinned it on her vest.

That's how Callie became the best sheriff in the whole Wild West. And that's how a little town got itself a brand-new name ...

Nice and Friendly Corners!

THE END

Milkshake Mystery

NOW THESE HERE MILKSHAKES MAY LOOK AND TASTE **DELICIOUS**, BUT SOMEONE HAS BEEN SLURPING AWAY AT THEM!

Can you help Ella re-arrange the glasses in order of how full they are? Number the glasses 1 to 5, making the fullest glass number 1 and the one with the least milkshake in it number 5.

a

b

c

d

e

Answers on page 66.

UH-OH, SOME COWS HAVE MADE A MESS RUNNING THROUGH TOWN. BOTH PICTURES LOOK THE SAME, BUT CAN YOU SPOT FIVE DIFFERENCES IN THE BOTTOM ONE?

Colour a sheriff badge each time you find a difference.

Answers on page 66.

Sheriff Callie's Wild West Quiz

HAVE FUN FINDING OUT HOW MUCH YOU KNOW ABOUT
SHERIFF CALLIE AND HER **ROOTIN' TOOTIN'** FRIENDS!

1 Can you match this detail to the right character?

ⓐ   ⓑ   ⓒ

2 What is the missing word?

Yipee-ki-yally!

IT'S SHERIFF _____!

3 Ella is famous in Nice and Friendly Corners for making the best ever:

ⓐ **Cookies**

ⓑ **Spaghetti**

ⓒ **Milkshakes**

4 Who does Sheriff Callie ride? Draw a circle around the right character.

a **b**

5 Uncle Bun is the owner of the Milk Saloon.

a True ☐

b False ☐

6 Who is Deputy Peck's best buddy?

Say his name out loud!

a **b**

Answers on page 66.

ANSWERS

**PAGES 8-9: INTRODUCING...
SHERIFF CALLIE**
PRIZE TRAIL – A MILKSHAKE.

PAGES 12-13: HOWDY, FOLKS!
SPARKY – A, TOBY – C, SHERIFF CALLIE – D,
DEPUTY PECK – B.
I SPY – CLEMENTINE IS KEEPING HER DISTANCE,
BEHIND DEPUTY PECK.

**PAGES 18-19: FOLLOW THE
FOOTSTEPS**
TRUE OR FALSE? – TRUE.

**PAGES 20-21: WILD WEST
TEASERS**
1. D, 3. C, 5. 5.

**PAGES 22-23: INTRODUCING ...
DEPUTY PECK**
HOPPIN' HATS – HAT B.

PAGES 24-25: GAME OVER
6 BLUE CARDS, 5 RED CARDS.
LASSO MAGIC – B.

PAGE 26: PAIR 'EM UP!
A AND F, B AND G, C AND E.
D IS THE ODD ONE OUT.
COLOUR CHECK – PINK.

PAGE 27: ALL IN A MUDDLE!
RUNNING FROM TOP TO BOTTOM: 4, 2, 3, 1, 6, 5.

PAGE 28: THE CACTUS CODE
TOBIAS P. CACTUS

PAGE 29: SPECIAL SPARKY
A HORSESHOE AND A CARROT.

PAGES 30-31: OUT AND ABOUT
1. FALSE. SHE IS RIDING SPARKY, 2. UNCLE BUN,
3. THE LASSO IS ON A PORCH, 4. HAPPY.

**PAGES 34-35: INTRODUCING ...
TOBY**
ODD ONE OUT – BARREL C.

PAGES 36-37: LEAPIN' LASSOS!
COLOUR CHECK – THE APPLE SHOULD
BE YELLOW.

PAGE 38: BRAVE THE MAZE!

PAGE 41: MIRROR MESSAGE
FRIEND TO ALL!

PAGE 45: PARTY TIME!
THERE ARE 3 MILKSHAKES IN THE PICTURE.

PAGE 50-51: SPRING WELCOME!
MATCH AND COLOUR
1 – BLUE, 2 – GREEN, 3 – YELLOW,
4 – PINK, 5 – PURPLE.

PAGE 52: PICTURE PUZZLES
1. C.
2. A – PECK, B – ELLA, C – TOBY.

PAGE 53: HEADING HOME
C. PECK AND TOBY ARE IN ELLA'S SALOON
WAITING TO SEE CALLIE.

PAGE 54-55: LET'S GO SHOPPING

PAGE 56-57: SHAPE UP!
1 – F, 2 – A, 3 – C, 4 – E, 5 – D, 6 – B.

PAGE 58: ODD ONE OUT
1 – C, 2 – A, 3 – B.
WHEELIE EASY – 3.

PAGE 62: MILKSHAKE MYSTERY
1 – D, 2 – A, 3 – E, 4 – B, 5 – C.

PAGE 63: WHAT'S CHANGED?

**PAGES 64-65: SHERIFF CALLIE'S
WILD WEST QUIZ**
1. B, 2. CALLIE, 3. C, 4. A, 5. B, 6. B – TOBY.

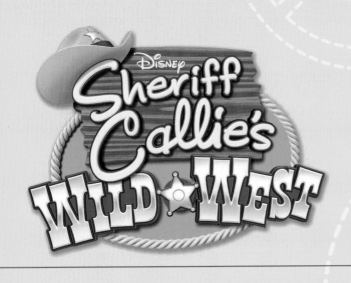

cutest
COWGIRL
in the Wild West!